Sam and His BIG Apple Harmonica

Written by: Ila Mary Osach

Illustrated by: Amy Rottinger

Halo
PUBLISHING
INTERNATIONAL

ISBN: 978-1-63765-122-3
LCCN: 2021919828

Halo Publishing International, LLC
www.halopublishing.com

Printed and bound in the United States of America

This book is dedicated to my dad, Sam Hauser,
and to every child who has a dream.

APPles!

4

Once upon a time, there lived a man in New York City. He was a very nice man, and he loved music. He also loved his harmonica. It was very special to him.

The man's name was Sam. Sam lived in New York City, known by many as the Big Apple. He'd lived there his whole life. New York is a big city, but Sam knew every street and avenue and loved to walk.

Although Sam lived in New York, he didn't have a house to call his own. Sam always lived with friends or family, but he wanted a home of his own. While he walked the streets thinking of how he could get one, he would always stop and joyfully play his harmonica.

Sam smiled at everyone he met walking. He was friendly, and people loved him. But he still needed a place to live. What was he to do?

Sam looked in his pocket and found a dime. Back then, a dime was worth more. The dime was all he had along with his harmonica, his very special harmonica that he loved to play.

He used the dime to buy a cup of coffee. Sam loved coffee, and back then, you could buy a cup for just a dime. Sam drank his coffee while sitting on a bench in New York City and thought about playing his harmonica. He realized, quite to his delight, that he could play his harmonica for people as they passed by. Then he had a brilliant idea!

He placed his empty coffee cup on the bench and started to play his favorite tunes on his favorite harmonica. Everyone that passed stopped for a while to listen. He was so delighted it put a great big smile on his face.

He noticed when he looked at his coffee cup, there was money in there. Wow, he was so happy that he was earning money by playing his harmonica for everyone that passed by. Every day, Sam would set up his coffee cup and play his harmonica. Many more people learned of Sam and his harmonica and would come every day to hear him play. As this caught on, he became more and more known around the city. Word spread. He was the talk of the town. The Big Apple was truly welcoming Sam and his harmonica.

And better yet, he was earning more and more money to save to one day buy his own place to live. Sam realized he could play his harmonica, which he loved, and earn money for something he loved to do. People noticed him and he was happy. He would choose different places in the city to play, and he became famous.

Sam continued to play his harmonica for everyone he met, and it always put a great big smile on his face. Better yet, he earned enough money to buy a house of his own.

He always knew his harmonica would bring him happiness and joy, and he shared those feelings with all who listened to his music. Sam never gave up on himself, and he was able to fulfill his dream of making people happy.

CPSIA information can be obtained
at www.ICGtesting.com
Printed in the USA
LVHW070433171121
703473LV00009B/488